For Jasper—J.S.

For my mother and father—M.S.

THIS IS A BORZOI BOOK PUBLISHED BY ALFRED A. KNOPF

Published in the United States of America by Alfred A. Knopf, an imprint of Random
House Children's Books, a division of Random House, Inc., New York, and simultaneously
in Canada by Random House of Canada Limited, Toronto. Distributed by Random
House, Inc., New York. KNOPF, BORZOI BOOKS, and the colophon are registered trademarks
of Random House, Inc.

www.randomhouse.com/kids

Library of Congress Cataloging-in-Publication Data
Schulman, Janet.
A bunny for all seasons / by Janet Schulman ; illustrated by Meilo So. — 1st ed.
p.   cm.
Summary: A little brown bunny enjoys visiting a garden from summer to spring,
especially when a gray bunny shares the fun.
ISBN 0-375-82256-9 (trade) — ISBN 0-375-92256-3 (lib. bdg.)
[1. Rabbits—Fiction. 2. Seasons—Fiction.] I. So, Meilo, ill. II. Title.
PZ7.S3866 Bu 2003
[E]—dc21
2002007289

Printed in the United States of America
January 2003
10 9 8 7 6 5 4 3 2 1
First Edition

A BUNNY FOR ALL SEASONS

By **JANET SCHULMAN**

Illustrated by MEILO SO

Alfred A. Knopf ✦ New York

One hot summer day a little brown bunny rabbit hopped out of the woods and into a garden.

Her nose quivered and sniffed. She smelled so many things to eat, she hardly knew where to start.

The carrot tops were very good, the lettuce even better, and the strawberries, oh, they were something special.

The bunny ate and ate until
she could eat no more.

Then she sniffed and hopped to the part of the garden with all the pretty flowers. What a wonderful garden someone has made just for me, she thought.

Every day that summer the bunny visited the garden. The yellow beans were a treat. She wasn't so sure about the big red tomatoes.

Some days an old cat would chase her,
but she was always faster.

In the fall the days got cooler and shorter, but there were
still cabbages and parsnip tops and radishes, all very tasty.

The bunny had grown bigger and now
her fur was getting thicker.

More leaves fell every day. There wasn't much left in the garden besides the big orange pumpkins.

She couldn't eat them,
but they were very
good to hide behind
when the cat came
slinking by.

Then early one morning she found a surprise by the
tool shed. It was another bunny, a gray bunny.

The two bunnies sniffed and hopped until their noses touched. The brown bunny was so happy. She had found a friend.

Winter came. The wind howled. The snow fell.
The two bunnies snuggled up together in their
burrow in the woods. All they had to eat was
bark from the smallest trees.

One moonlit night the two bunnies went to the
garden. They hopped and danced and played
chase on the snow-covered lawn around the
garden, just for the fun of it.

On the first warm day of spring, the brown bunny went to the garden. She sampled the green shoots popping up around the crocuses. Then she bit off the tenderest ones, made sure the cat was sound asleep, and hopped back to her burrow.

In a little while the brown bunny returned.
The gray bunny came too. And guess what
came with them?

Their three new little bunnies!

All spring long the baby bunnies ate delicious daffodil and tulip leaves under the watchful eyes of daddy and mommy bunny.

Could it *ever* get better? Oh, yes, just wait until summer, their mommy promised. And so it was.